IT'S RAINING,
IT'S POURING

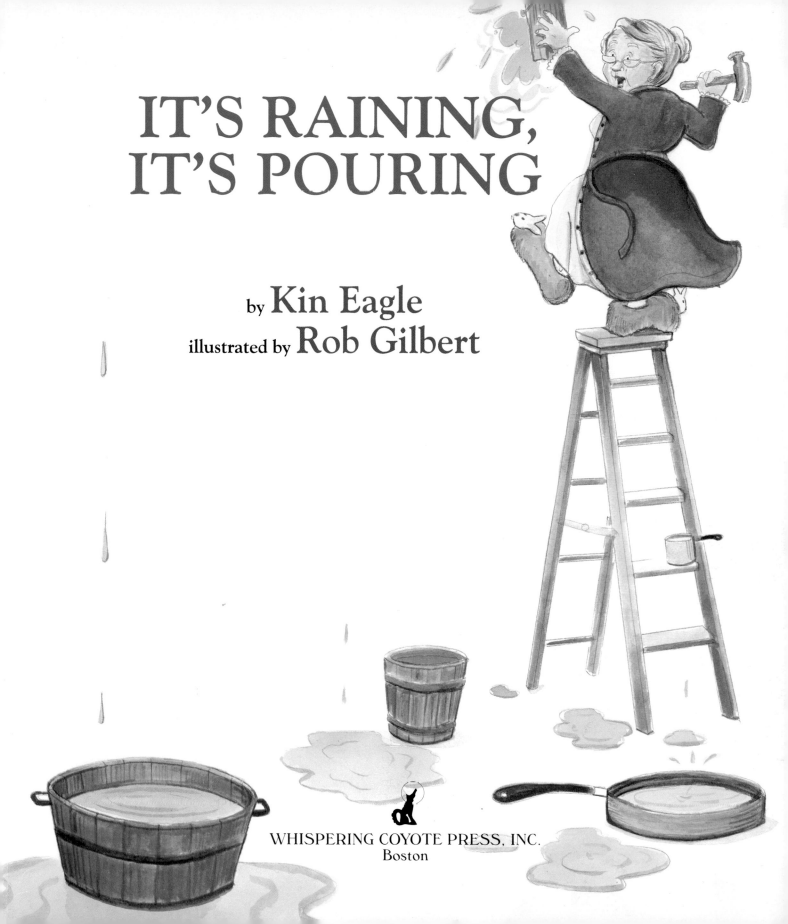

IT'S RAINING,
IT'S POURING

by **Kin Eagle**

illustrated by **Rob Gilbert**

WHISPERING COYOTE PRESS, INC.
Boston

Special thanks to Kim and Dan Adlerman
and to Cecilia Laureys, without whose help
this book would not have been possible
—R.G.

An Our House Book

Published by Whispering Coyote Press, Inc.
480 Newbury Street, Suite 104, Danvers, MA 01923
Text copyright © 1994 by Kin Eagle
Illustrations copyright © 1994 by Rob Gilbert
Printed in Hong Kong by South China Printing Company (1988) Ltd.
Book production and design by Our House

First edition
10 9 8 7 6 5 4 3 2 1

Library of Congress Cataloging-in-Publication Data
Eagle, Kin, 1964-
It's raining, it's pouring / written by Kin Eagle ; illustrated by Rob Gilbert.
p.   cm.
Summary: This expanded version of the nursery rhyme "It's raining, it's pouring" shows what hap-
pens to the old man in all kinds of weather.
ISBN 1-879085-88-7 ; $14.95
[1. Weather—Fiction. 2. Stories in rhyme.] I. Gilbert, Roby, ill. II. Title.
PZ8.3.E112515It 1994
[E]—dc20   93-40897

For my parents
—K.E.

For Mao, Poppy, and Georgia
—R.G.

It's raining, it's pouring,
the old man is snoring.

He bumped his head
when he went to bed
and couldn't get up in the morning.

It's cloudy, it's breezy,
the old man is sneezy.

He blew so hard
that he moved the stars,
but of course that wasn't easy!

It's snowing, it's blowing,
the old man is growing.

He ate so much
one day for lunch
every part of him was showing.

It's warm out and sunny.
The old man loves honey.

He tried to seize
a batch from the bees
and they didn't find it funny.

It's cool, damp, and chilly.
The old man's name is Willy.

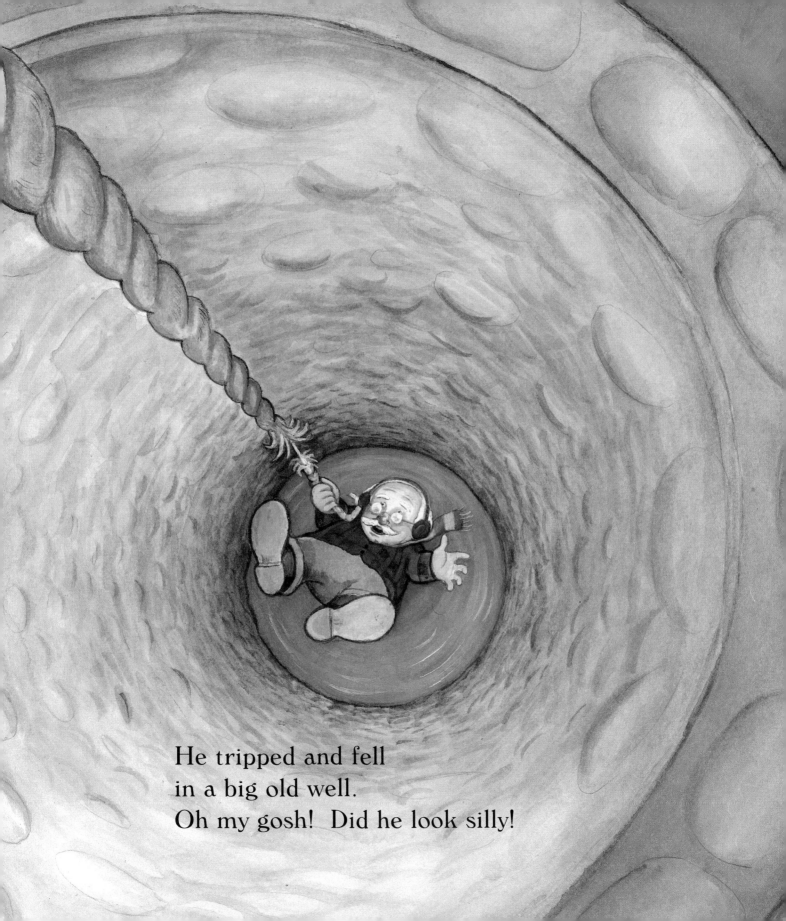

He tripped and fell
in a big old well.
Oh my gosh! Did he look silly!

It's gusty, it's windy.
The old man's wife is Cindy.

With ants in their pants
they started to dance,
and ended up doing the Lindy.

Whatever the season—
cloudy, sunny, breezin'—
if he gets to bed
without bumping his head,
then the old man thinks it's pleasin'.

It's Raining, It's Pouring

It's rain - ing, it's pour - ing, the old man is snor - ing. He

bumped his head when he went to bed and could-n't get up in the morn - ing.

2. It's cloudy, it's breezy,
the old man is sneezy.
He blew so hard
that he moved the stars,
but of course *that* wasn't easy!

3. It's snowing, it's blowing,
the old man is growing.
He ate so much
one day for lunch
every part of him was showing.

4. It's warm out and sunny.
The old man loves honey.
He tried to seize
a batch from the bees
and they didn't find it funny.

5. It's cool, damp, and chilly.
The old man's name is Willy.
He tripped and fell
in a big old well.
Oh my gosh! Did he look silly!

6. It's gusty, it's windy.
The old man's wife is Cindy.
With ants in their pants
they started to dance,
and ended up doing the Lindy.

7. Whatever the season—
cloudy, sunny, breezin'–
if he gets to bed
without bumping his head,
then the old man thinks it's pleasin'.